It started out so "innocently" - just a way to pay for some books for their beloved school.
Now these three teachers have taken their unique funding plans to new heights.
So during Spring Recess, they take over and run an...
The bid is at $2000 for Daphne! Going-going-GONE! "Mr Blue", she's all yours!
I have $2100 NOW $2200...any more bidders for the lovely Donna? All done at $2200!
Well done Mr. Yellow!
And for Roz, the bid is 2100! Do I hear 2100? I have 2400!
All in at $2,400! 2,400 dollars for Mr. Orange!
Auction!
That ends our first round auction, gentlemen! These ladies will now retire to their respective rooms and get ready for some good "clean" fun!
Those of you who did not win this round will be able to enjoy the action on these three state-of-the-art screens!
And for a mere $300 each, DVDs will be available to anyone who'd like to relive the experience!

Let's start the show on our main stage with Donna and the *lucky* Mr Yellow!
It seems you don't suffer from "*stage fright*" Mr. Yellow!
No! <Suck!> I *love* a good crowd!
Oh my! We should call you "*Mr Throbbing Purple*"!

Let's pretend we're alone!
uhhh... my balls...
I want you *all* to myself!
uhhhh...
<glort>
Since I was a boy, my *fantasy* was to fuck a teacher!
Now, to think my *dream* has come true! And I get to take a DVD of it home!
Just don't let "*Mrs Yellow*" see it!

Get these panties off!
I want to see that pussy!
Suck my cock, you little whore!
While I rub your clit!
What a delightful little asshole you have!
Very nice!
Sweet!
Eat that ass!
The teacher becomes the student!

Meanwhile, in the library.
Ah, Mr Blue...
You're *just* in time!
I can't seem to find "*The Glories of Heaven*"
It's the *first* place I'd look!
Have you looked *here?*
Oh, Mr Blue!
Why would I keep "*The Glories of Heaven*" in my *panties?*
In fact, I'll be happy to *keep* looking!
Well! It's nice to have help in the library!

No one's here! You can be as *loud* as you like!
<*slurp!*> Your pussy is so sweet!
I want you naked!
I want to lick *every* inch of your body!
Then they're fuckin' idiots! Oooohh...
My *other* students tend to sit around and text their friends!

If you were MY teacher, I'd never take my eyes off you!
Well, you know kids today...too many distractions!
Ummm...you've got ALL my attention!
So I can tell...
This cock of yours is at full alert!
It's so thick and hard and ready!

Oh yeah! She's gonna take **ALL** of that!
Let's hear it for ***Daphne***, gentlemen!
Beautiful mouth!
Such a pro!
Oh, yeah...
Hmmm!
She's ***really*** enjoying it!
Can I get a tissue here?
Cum in my mouth!
Your asshole is like candy!

Every part of you is delicious!
Slide that monster in deep!
Oh! oooh! OHHH!
OOOH!!
OOOH!!
OOOHH!
Humm!
UHHHH!
Who's got the tissues?

fuuuck...
Great tits!
Thanks! They're real!
Hard to find these days!
Your pussy is so tight and wet!
That's 'cause your dick is so fuckin' huge!
It's like getting pounded by a novelty dildo..
with a real guy attached on the other end!!
hmmm... Flattery will get you a dick in the ass!

Naked! Lets get naked!!!
Easy there, Speed Racer!
Take your time...get your money's worth!
We've got each other...
And an audience...
to entertain!
Hello Mister Stand-up!

I'm *definitely* going to have fun with *this!*
Oh! They're looking *right* at me!
Watching me *suck* your *cock!*
uhhh...my balls! Do my balls!
<*slorp*>! Like this?
OoooH fuck yessss...
Suck them *hard!* OOH!

Oh Christ! Both of them! *YESSs!*
Now I'm gonna fuck you senseless!
Big words, big man! *Bring it!*

Let's hear it for these little ladies, gents? Aren't they *wild?!*
Magnificent!
Let's get *another* auction started!
Outstanding!
It's been more than 4 hours! I should call my doctor!

I can't ***believe*** how much money we're making!
And so ***fast!***
This'll keep the school going for the entire year!
I've ***never*** been happier to be in charge of the dressing room!
Thank God all our faces will be digitally blurred! If these sessions ever got out onto the web unaltered, we'd ***really*** be fucked!
Yeah...that'd make Parent-Teacher night a little tough to manage!

Gentlemen, *what* can I say?
You've *seen* them in action!
You *know* what they can do!
And these *asses?* They speak pure poetry!
Our next auction will be for *all-anal* access!

Roz!
$3,500!
$4,000!
$4,500!
$5,000!
$5,500!
$6,000!
Daphne!
$6,000!
$7,000!
Donna!
$5,000!
Congratulation to the winning ass-bandits! Money *well spent*, gentlemen!
You can proceed to the marked doors, where your ladies await!

Mr. Green! You've won the honor of pounding Roz between the cheeks!
Mr. Red! You get full back-door Donna privileges!
And of course, Mr. Brown, with a name like that...
Daphne's delightful little asshole is all yours!
Would you believe I've never taken it up the butt?
No...but you're sweet to say that!
We're in for supreme ass-wrecking tonight!
You are so hot!
Kiss me!
Hummm!

Where are we going?
This is our spot!
The broom closet! It's dark and tight...just like my ass!
Only the janitor's been here too!
Ha! Cute!
Be gentle please.
No promises...
Ho-leee Fuck!

classy…
I'm a *dirty* little girl!
Ooh yeah!
You *really* are!
Shit! It's so fuckin' thick!
Take it! Take every inch!
You are *SO* nasty!
You're damned right I am!

Pretty sure they put some mattresses out here.
Let's have a look...
Sweet Jesus! I'm doubling up on the dick pills!
What an ass!
Beautiful!
I like that...touch me *right there!*

Those lil' blue pills are startin' to kick in!
So they *are!* Isn't modern medicine wonderful?
I want your ass so bad!
It's all yours, lover!
Let's spark this fella up!
Oh yeah! He's *rarin'* to go!
Give me your ass!
Spread your legs! Let me *see* that asshole!
Lubed and ready for you!

Get it... in there...
OW! Oh!
More?
Yes! Oh, yeah!
So tight!
Hurts so good!
Surprise!
Tony?
What are you doing here?
Enjoying the show!
Oh!

Hello? I'm still here!
Hmm? Oh, yes, of course!
Sweetie, I'm kinda in the middle of something here!
I know! I'm one of tonight's cameramen!
Didn't have enough money to get in front of the camera!
I think we can afford some "Pro Bono" work!
And that's a fine "Bono"!

I mean, we *are* doing all this for charity. The *least* I can do is share a little school spirit on the side!
And you *do* fill me...
with more than spirit!
Put it in my ass!
Seriously?
Oh yes!
Wow! You're *really* flexible!
And your dick is even *bigger* than Mr. Brown's!

Still here, you know!
But keep at it!
You young folk...
Do it so well!
This goes into my personal collection! Smile!
I don't want to get us in trouble, but I think I ran out of tape about 2 hours ago...
That's fine. He'll just have to come back next year!
THE END!

ENRIQUE
VillAGRÁN

In every paradise lives a snake. That snake's name is Mojo - the local pirate, pimp, drug lord, entertainer, and unofficial mayor of the island.
He's currently enjoying his latest "*acquisition*".
You're *mine* now!
Oh yes!

How Daphne lost her Mojo (and got it back!)

Very much yours...
Give me all your cock!

I think she's a keeper!
Yeah. He's not letting her go!
Who's pussy is this?
Yours!
Louder, bitch!
Yours! It's your pussy!
You damned right it's mine!
Oh baby, you knock me out!
5 bottles of rum! Hmph! Who's the pussy now?
This would be my cue...
to get the fuck out of Dodge...
The guard is also out for the count! Good!
And the tide is low! Perfect!
Later much for all of this!

I've been all over this island! Where the hell could she have gotten to?
Really don't want to involve local law...
huh... naked girl... cute...
Holy shit! Daphne!
Wait! Daphne!
Serge! Thank God! I've escaped from Mojo and the pirates! You've got to hide me!
And you've got to get me some clothes!
Well, I've got to hide you...for starters!
I've got a shack nearby. Let's walk close to the surf to lose our footprints.
Oh, that's clever! You've done this before?
Angry husbands make fierce trackers!

A while later...
Mojo doesn't strike me as the "*cheerful loser*" type!
I've got a plan.
There's a bus that leaves tonight and can take you to your friend's house
You can hide there for a few days until you can take a plane home.
So... I won't see again...
Not for a ***long*** time.
So let's make the ***most*** of it!
This outfit will do!
Big floppy hat should hide my face.
Glad I still have the lucky anklet.

Here's your ride. Just try to blend in with the rest of the tourists. It's a long trip, so do your best to get some sleep.
Your ticket is for the upper deck, little missy.
TICKET 3A
Thank you.
Oh! No, *thank you!*
Let me help you with your bag, and *please* accept this drink on behalf of the company.

Take your seat please, we're pullin' out.
<shluurp> Oh, sure.
You're all squared away!
'scuse me - gotta get through
My seat's next to the window. Wow... *tight* squeeze!
I'm gonna try to get some sleep.
Okay. I'll be right here if you need *anything*
Anything at all!
Like rubbing your dick into my face?
Well aren't you sweet?

Got to admit...that was a *pretty stiff dick!*
And this drink is making me *hot* again!
Hey! Those toes are cold!
But they know what they're doing!
Ta-daa!
I think we have a stowaway!
Aw hell, he goes *everywhere* with me! We've traveled all over the world together!

Nice to meet the "both" of you!
I've got a spot...
Neither of you have ever been to!
Fuck me!
But quietly!
Wouldn't want you two to lose your job!
That's mighty thoughtful of you..?
Daphne. And you are..?
So glad I took tonight's shift!
Oh! Name's Doug.

Well *hel-lo* Doug!
I've never been fucked in a bus!
Welcome to the *"3-foot high club!"*
tee-hee! Good one!
Ohh...you've come.
You think your little friend's got anything left in the tank?
Hell yeah!
Then do me in the ass!
Well, you ask so nicely...
Ohh!

Best Goddamn piece of ass I've ever been in!
fuckmefuckme... *oh shit...* deeper!
Oh...God...now *that's* the way to pass the time...
I should travel by bus more often!
The next morning at Therese's
It's so good to have you back!
Let's have a toast with an extra-large Pokococo Shumbaya
Oh good! Just what I need! Something to make me even *hornier!*

You know the *active* ingredient...
in that drink...
Makes *good* sex great, and *great* sex...
Un-be-fuckin'-levible!

Uhhhh! <slurp>! This is so hot!
I love to eat your pussy!
Ohmygod! We...we've got to take a break!
<slurp>! Agreed!
And I'm going to need some money to get back home!
No worries. We'll go into town. After one more drink!
Sweety, the markets are over there.
I'm already shopping!
For large hairy tourists in Speedos?
Actually, Ari and his friend are jewelry dealers on vacation!

You can't get *anything* 'til we hit the ATM.
I'm just looking!
You like what you see?
The good stuff's in my *pants*!
Come behind the curtains, we'll show you *everything* we've got!
Wow! I can't leave you alone for a minute!
What? I'm getting a sales pitch!

Well at least keep the receipt!
It's...oh! It's called "bartering"!
uh-huh...
So who needs an ATM?
You're ready to max out your "Pussy Express!"
Never leave home without it!
How much is *this*?
I'd do *anything* for those pearls!
Anything!
!
That guy back there -
Did he hear me?
People on the *next island* heard you!
Do you like my boat?
Your what? Oh yes! <glorp>!

It's getting late, and my husband might get suspicious!
Husband? You *never* said...
But thanks a bunch for the necklace!
Oh...er... my pleasure!
Look at the time! *Must* dash!
That night..
Aren't *you* quite the little entrepreneur?
Had to raise funds *somehow*. And I didn't want to take all *your* money!
Besides, the faster I get the cash...
the quicker I'll be off Mojo's radar!

Back home at Thereses's
This should be enough to sell.
Then you can get off this island and away from Mojo!
This has been the weirdest trip I've ever had in *my life!*
I don't think it could *get* any stranger!
Surprise!
But...who?
His name's Brodsky.
An associate of my husband's.
He's had me looking for you ever since the craziness at Mojo's show!*
I got bored waiting, decided to save myself!
But since you're here... make yourself useful!
*See "Teach Me 3"

Everyone lost their shirts to Mojo! Your husband had to get back to the States.
Turns out, Prince Mojo's been runnin' his con for years down here!
Whoa! Watch the teeth ladies!
Okay! Nice working with class folk!
Let's go. I've got a yacht waiting for us!
Good! Let's get the hell out!
Hang on!
Okay if I hang on to this?
Sure...if you don't mind me losing my mind!
Oh wow! I grab it...
and it makes the bike go faster!
WEEEEE!
CHRIST!

Boat's paid up for the next two weeks...no sense in rushing home, right?
You like taking advantage of my husband, don't you?
I'm sorry. Does the club only allow *one member?*
Ha-ha! Very funny!
I take advantage of *any* opportunity I get!
And *you* are the golden ticket!
Oh! Feels like you're about to...
...explode!
BOOOM!
SPLASH
What the *fuck* was *that?!*
Nice shot Mike!
It's all in the wrist!
Stop or we'll sink you! We're coming aboard!

Hope we're not interrupting anything!
Pirates? Seriously?!
These are dangerous waters!
Don't tell me that...
Arrr! 'tis Mojo... Prince Mojo!
Did you really think you could escape me?
How the hell?
My dark mystic arts darlin'! And the tiny GPS chip I put in your anklet!
I do love modern technology!
Brodsky here will give over the money and the boat, and will continue taping your little sexual escapades!
Fine!

Back on the pirate boat...
Admit it! You've *never* had so much fun!
Oooh. Yes! It's true!
Your husband is more concerned for his money than his *delicious* wife!
Me? I would *never* let you go!
Oh...Prince Mojo!
Your ass belongs to *me!*
Agreed!
And so do your tits!
Yes! It's all yours!

And your dick...
is all mine! <glorp>!
<glock> <GLORK>
Fuck her hard! Show her husband what he's given up!
I *did* miss you.
That little asshole of her's looks lonely!

You wanna fuck my ass?
It does belong to me!
Let's make a clear path!
So you can stick it in!
Is that good for you?!
Nice and tight!
Daphne, I think you've got the crowd all worked up!

I *do* love an audience!
Look at you! **So perfect!**
I going to fuck you all night long!
Fuck yes! **Oooh!** Yeah!
AWWK! Fuck her butt! Fuck her butt!

You like having your ass fucked by *royalty?*
OW! Oh yeah!
Someone else grab the camera!
I want in on *this!*
It's a pirate's life for *me* too!
AWWK! Clusterfuck! Everybody fucks! *AWWK!*

Here's a little gift from Mojo himself!
You *are* the romantic! I love it!
It's *good* to be Mojo!
Now *everybody* fuck!
THE END!

I *do* wish your mother had given me more warning about your visit, darling!
My sister... *such a* - well, you know!
As much as I'd *love* to show you around the new place, I've a client in Paris *I simply have* to meet with!
You understand, don't you darling? Auntie Lu loves you so, but this meeting's taken 4 months to set up!
It's okay! I'm out of school and *not* with Mom! I'm a happy camper!

Young Daphne's Education Vacation!

Oh good! And Albert should be showing up soon. That's my new husband, and *your* new uncle!
Helen's our housekeeper. She'll help you with *anything* you need.
Antonio's our driver. He can take you to the mall or to the village with one of the cars.

I can't get over how grown-up you are! We're the same size!
Which is good, because we can't have you in these silly schoolgirl outfits!
Wear my stuff for now. When I get back...
We'll do some serious shopping!
And get you a decent hairstyle!
Honestly - your mother...
Oh no! I'm stuffed!
I think I'll just grab a shower!
You like my cooking? You want anything else?
You are now the lady of the house! You should have a lovely bath!
I can even give you a nice waxing!
But my legs are...
oh! You mean...
I do it for your Aunt.
I am very professional!
ow! ow! OWWW!
SHRRRIP!
Back there too?!
SHRRRRIP!
The bath will make you feel better!
Ahhh... yea, that is nice!

Oh yes! Very very smooth! Like baby's bottom!
Later, in Auntie Lu's closet...
Well now! Auntie Lu's got some nice items!
Beats the "granny panties" they make us wear at school!
She's right! We are the same size!
Mom would flip if she saw...
her little Daphne...
All grown-up!
Some make-up and a little more attention to the hair...

Ready for fashion week!
Ooo! Satin on freshly-waxed puss! *Yes!*
I think this is Madam's private closet, dear. There are things in here you should not see!
C'mon! I've seen lacy underwear before!
That's *not* what I was referring to...
Whoa! Is that what I *think* it is?
You're a big girl now. I'm sure you *know* what this is.
It's *huge*, I know that!

Put it in your mouth.
Really? But it's buzzing!
That just means it's happy to see you!
I put it here, and now *you're* happy to see it!
Oh, I...I don't know!
But I've never...
You go to an ***all-girl*** school!
Stop teasing me!
Okay, ***once!*** With Janet in gym class!
But it was a ***dare!*** We just kissed!
Open your legs Daphne, I have ***something*** for you!
I...I don't ***mmmmm!***

Feels good, *doesn't it?* So hard!
Oh my *God!*
I'm going to go in a little deeper!
Oh! Okay! *Deeper!*
You like it?
Oh *hell* yes!
Here I thought I'd get to enjoy our guest *first!*
My dear Helen. Such an impatient little whore!
I'll get *my* turn soon enough...

I have another surprise for you Daphne!
Really? What?
Antonio will show you!
I think you'll enjoy it!
Miss Daphne, you're looking quite beautiful!
Helen says you're in for a surprise!
Where're we going?
Helen didn't really dress me for the mall!
Don't worry, what you're wearing is *perfect*!
We're here! Go ahead in!
I'm the surprise Daphne!
Oh my God, it's ***bigger*** than Helen's!

Well, *mine* doesn't have batteries either...
But it's 100% genuine cock!
Go ahead. *Touch it!*
It's so heavy! And warm!
Now suck it!
Feel how it pulsates?
Uh-oh! Something's... uh...happening! *<glorp>!*
I'm coming! *Swallow it!*

Are you *sure* this is the first time you've ever done that?
Uh-huh! Guess I'm a natural!
You've got a talent! It must run in the family!
Hey! It's getting hard *again*!
Take your clothes off!
Okay. Just don't rip them! They're not mine!
Spread yourself open!
This is a little embarrassing!
Nonsense! You're a magnificent creature!
I really like your cock!

You're all waxed! Helen?
Yes! She insisted!
I'll have to thank her!
Ummm... fuck me first!
Slow but hard.
Oh!
I want you to remember every inch!
Oh, my God!
You should always remember your first!
Oh! oh! OOOH!
Antonio!

So far... BEST vacation *ever!*
I'm glad!
What is this place?
This is your Uncle Albert's hideaway!
Before he married your Aunt, he'd take all his "*lady friends*" there!
Oh...he's a *lot* of fun!
I haven't met him yet. He *sounds* like a fun guy!
Good, they're back!
My friends are *never* gonna believe this!
Well then, we should take some pictures!
An *excellent* idea!

Fantastic!
Look into the camera!
You're a dirty girl!
Push her face into your pussy!
Suck my cock!
Spread that ass!

And now... the money shot!
This will be a fucking masterpiece!
Suck it! *Suck it! OhhhH!*
<GLORK> <glaggg> <SLORP>
Take it! Take it *deep!*

The following morning.
Lu's niece! What the hell am I supposed to do with her?
Do I take her shopping? Nah, that's Lu's department!
I'm no good with little kids! Shit! I'm drawing a blank!
Christ. Maybe I can tip the staff to keep her amused!
The one time my flight is early, and I've got this to deal with!
Fishing?
Hiking?
Horseback riding?
The hell do I do with...
a little girl?!?
Check out the wig! How cool is this?
Looks very grown-up!
You could pass for 25, easily!
That is no little girl!
But the staff is keeping her amused!

I'm gonna get some more coff...Oh!
Hello! You must be Daphne!
I'm your Uncle Albert. Lu said you were pretty, but...*Wow!*
Gee... thanks!
Let's have a kiss for Uncle Al!
Oh! You're right! Silly me! <smak>
Does Lu know you've invaded her closet?
She said to go ahead! This isn't my hair either!
So, I've *got* to ask, how *old are you?*
Just turned 18, Why?
Legal reasons...

I want to show you my cabin, but you *have* to be of legal age!
Will we be drinking there?
We're gonna work up a thirst!
OOOOO! Sounds like more fun!
And so...
Bet you've *never* been to a cabin like this
I might have.
Once.
Long time ago!
I'm a little chilly.
We can't have *that!* Let me warm you up!
Is that better?
My feet are *freezing!*

Put them here, they'll warm faster.
There?
Oh yes! Rub them around!
Like this?
Oh that's perfect!
It's getting a lot warmer!
And harder!
Wow! What's *in there?*
Check it out!
And it does *more* than warm toes!

I wonder if I can...
Did your Aunt teach you this?!
Nope! Just seems like a fun idea!
Oh! Yeah! Fun! Wow!
This is fun too!

Do we tell Aunt Lu?
I don't think so.
Let's just keep this our little adventure!
"Adventure" I like that!
You like adventure?
Sure! This vacation's been the best adventure ever!
Well here's a little twist for you...
Turn over.
I'm gonna fuck your ass!
What for?

That's... OWWW!
A little too OWWW!
Much adVENture! OOHHH!
Relax honey...
There it goes! Ohh!
Ah! Yeah! Oooh!
Aunt Lu gets back in 3 days...
You think we'll be done by then?
THE END!